This book belongs to:

....

For Tiggers & Dad
S/xx

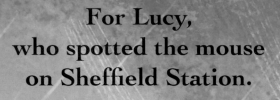

For Lucy,
who spotted the mouse
on Sheffield Station.

P.B.

First published in 2013 by Hodder Children's Books
This paperback edition published in 2014

Text © Peter Bently 2013
Illustrations © Steve Cox 2013

Hodder Children's Books,
338 Euston Road, London, NW1 3BH
Hodder Children's Books Australia,
Level 17/207 Kent Street, Sydney, NSW 2000

A catalogue record of this book is
available from the British Library.

ISBN 978 1 444 91021 6

10 9 8 7 6 5 4 3 2 1

Printed in China

Hodder Children's Books is a
division of Hachette Children's Books,
an Hachette UK Company

www.hachette.co.uk

LITTLE WALLOP

The Cat, the Mouse and the Runaway Train

Peter Bently & Steve Cox

LITTLE WALLOP

Hodder Children's Books

A division of Hachette Children's Books

This is the **skittery-scattery** mouse
Who lives in the stationmaster's house.

This is Carruthers, the station cat,
Who sleeps in the stationmaster's hat.

This is the cat when he suddenly sees,
Stealing a slice of his master's cheese,

The **skittery-scattery scurrying** mouse
Scuttling back to her
skirting board
house.

She **slips** and she **stumbles**
and **SNIPPETY SNAP!**
She's caught in the
stationmaster's trap!

This is the stationmaster, Pete,
Giving Carruthers a pat
    and a treat.
'I'm putting that mouse
    on the **ten** o'clock train.
She won't ever nibble
    my cheddar again!'

This is the box as it drops to the floor –
It's **9:52** and she's off through the door!

LUGGAGE

4

5

6

FRAGILE

This is the **scooting**, **skedaddling** mouse,
Heading back home to her skirting board house.

LITTLE WALLOP

Look at the shock on the pussycat's face.
It's **9:53** and Carruthers gives chase!

This is the mouse with the cat on her tail,
It's **9:54** and she's **leaping** the rail...

This is the cat as he **stumbles** and *reels*,
Tripping and *tumbling* head over heels.

It's **9:55** and Carruthers is **stuck!**
The mouse is delighted.
What excellent luck!

This is the train as it tears down the track,

Huffity-chuffity, clickety-clack.

This is the driver, Bartholomew Blake,
Trying and trying to pull on the brake.

The brake doesn't work
and the signal's on **red!**

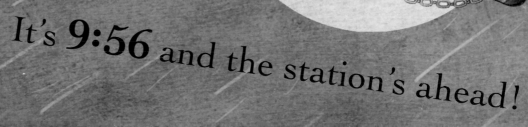

It's **9:56** and the station's ahead!

This is the mouse as she hears through the rain,

At **9:57**, the runaway train.

'Mouse!' cries Carruthers.

'Oh, please **stop the train!**

I promise I won't ever chase you again!'

This is the mouse in a *skittling scurry*,
It's **9:58**! Oh hurry, mouse, hurry!

Back over sleepers
and slippery track,

Up to the signal box,

in through a crack.

This is our Pete nodding off in a doze.
It's **9:59** as she tickles his nose –

Atishoo! Atishoo!
He wakes with a sneeze.
And **leaps** to his feet
as he instantly sees –

LITTLE WALLOP

Thundering Thaddeus! Heck and tarnation –
The runaway train heading into the station!

This is Pete **leaping** and **seizing** a lever, **Heaving** it back in a *frenzy* and *fever*.

And switches the train to a different track!

It **steams** down a siding – the brakes work at last!

It **squeals** to a halt
and the danger is past.

Meeooow!

LITTLE WALLOP